Why me God? Why me?

David E. Thomley

To order additional copies of this book, contact:
Xlibris
844-714-8691
www.Xlibris.com
Orders@Xlibris.com

ISBN: Softcover   979-8-3694-1527-6
        EBook   979-8-3694-1528-3

Library of Congress Control Number: 2024901453

Print information available on the last page

Rev. date: 01/22/2024

Why me God? Why me?

Why me God? Why me? Is a children's short story that highlights a young person who questions why God allows them to be treated so differently, and at times so mean. The story brings to light many issues children are confronted with daily. In the end, you will discover the answer to the question that is asked many times throughout the book.

Why are people so mean? Why do people call me names and make fun of me? Why do some people think I am weird just because I don't like the same things they like?

Sometimes I feel like giving up, sometimes I feel so sad because people make me feel like I don't even matter. Sometimes I just have to ask; Why me God? Why me?

Kids at my school make fun of the way I look. Why me God?

Kids on the playground make fun of me during PE class
because I sit on a bench and read.

People at the mall make fun of me because of the way
I dress. Why me God? Why me?

Kids in my dance class make fun of me because I am a terrible dancer. Why me God?

My classmates laugh at me in gym class because I am
not very athletic. Why me God?

The kids on my school bus make fun of me because I am so quiet. Why me God? Why me?

I think people are always staring at me because I am overweight. Why me God?

Sometimes people at school bully me. Why me God?
Why Me?

I fell off of my bicycle and broke my arm. Why me God?

My heart was broken when my little dog Mercy was hit by a car. Why me God?

I was so sad when my grandfather passed away, I didn't understand why he had to leave us so soon. Why me God? Why me?

When my dad had to leave for the Army I was sad and depressed. Why me God?

Why me God? Why Me? Well Why not me God? I am one of your children and I know you love me. God I pray you will always be with me, I pray you will protect me, and give me strength to face anything that comes my way. Amen

Jesus said,

"Let the little children come to me, and do not hinder them,
for the kingdom of heaven belongs to such as these."

Matthew 19:14

Printed in the United States
by Baker & Taylor Publisher Services